Shopping at the Mall

written by:

Kathleen Urmston
Karen Evans

illustrated by:

Barbara Dragony

KAEDEN ❤ BOOKS™

Mom and I went shopping
at the mall.
We had fun together.
At the shoe store we bought
a pair of gym shoes.

At the sports store we bought a pair of socks.
I need them for gym class.

Mom and I went shopping
at the mall.
We had fun together.
At the card store we bought
a birthday card
and wrapping paper.

At the toy store we bought a doll.
My sister's birthday is next week.

Mom and I went shopping
at the mall.
We had fun together.
At the department store we bough
a new dress.

At the drug store we bought
red nail polish.
Mom is going out tonight.

DRUG STORE

On the way home we stopped
at the ice cream store.
We bought ice cream cones.
I love chocolate ice cream.

Mom and I went shopping
at the mall.
We had fun together.

ICE CREAM